Written by Sheila Higginson

Illustrated by the Imaginism Studio
and the Disney Storybook Art Team

Ashland, OH 44805
www.bendonpub.com

© Disney

This is **VAMPIRINA HAUNTLEY**.
Her family calls her Vee. You can, too!

Boris and Oxana are Vee's dad and mom.
They are very proud of their little girl!

The Hauntleys are a
little **DIFFERENT** from most families.

Can you guess why?
Connect the dots to see what makes them special.

VEE IS A VAMPIRE!

She lives in Transylvania.
She has lots of **COOL** monster friends there.

VAMPIRINA HAUNTLEY

How many words can you make
from the letters in Vampirina Hauntley?

_____   _____

_____   _____

_____   _____

_____   _____

_____   _____

_____

_____

_____

_____

She has other friends, too.
Demi is the **GHOST** who haunts Vee's house.

HOW MANY?

Count the bats. How many do you see?

Your
Answer

MISSING PIECE

Circle the missing piece of the puzzle.

1

2

3

OXANA

Using the grid as a guide, draw the character in the box below.

SHADOW MATCH

Which shadow matches Vee?

A

B

C

Your
Answer

© Disney

Chef Remy is the family chef who cooks
the **SPOOKIEST** meals in Transylvania!

© Disney

TRANSYLVANIA

How many words can you make
from the letters in Transylvania?

_____   _____

_____   _____

_____   _____

_____   _____

_____

_____

_____

_____

_____

WHICH ARE THE SAME?

Which two images are the same?

A

B

C

D

Your
Answer

Wolfie is the family pet.

SHADOW MATCH

Which shadow matches Wolfie?

Your
Answer

A

B

C

WHICH ARE THE SAME?

Which two images are the same?

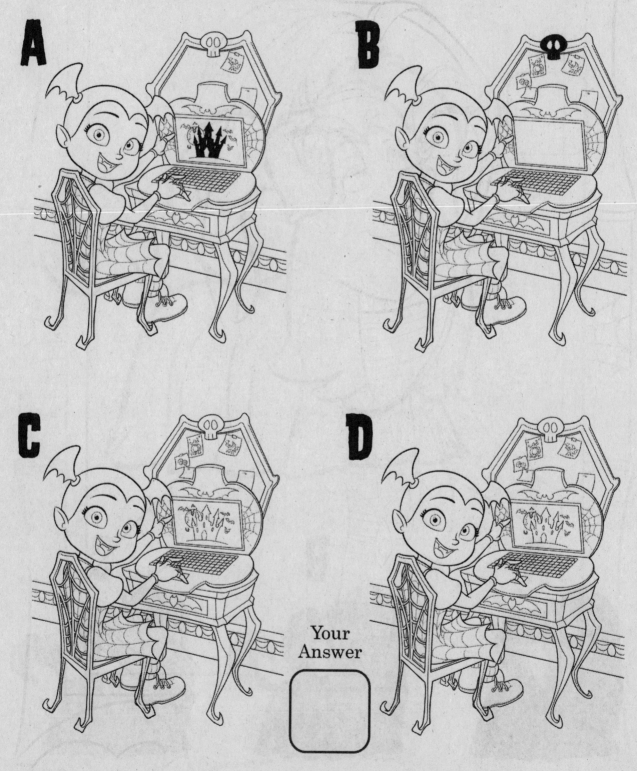

A

B

C

D

Your
Answer

Oxana

Boris and Oxana have a surprise for Vee.
Use the code to find out what the message says.

Answer: WE ARE MOVING!

The Hauntleys are **MOVING** to Pennsylvania!

© Disney

HOW MANY?

Count the ghost. How many do you see?

Your
Answer

They're going to live in their Great Uncle Dieter's house.

"It's going to be a family adventure!" Boris tells Vee.

Draw a picture of Vee saying good-bye to her friends.

SHADOW MATCH

Which shadow matches Vee?

A

B

C

Your
Answer

HOW MANY?

Count the moons. How many do you see?

Your
Answer

"It sure looks **SPOOKY** in here," Vee says.
"It feels like home!"

There are 6 differences between the two pictures of Vee's new bedroom. Can you find them?

DEMI

Using the grid as a guide,
draw the character in the
box below.

MISSING PIECE

Circle the missing piece of the puzzle.

1

2

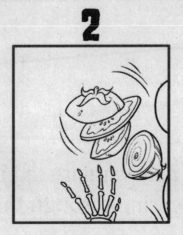

3

Vee and Demi play vampire tag in the new house.
"No fair disappearing through things!" Vee shouts.

FOLLOW THE PATH

Which path leads to Boris?

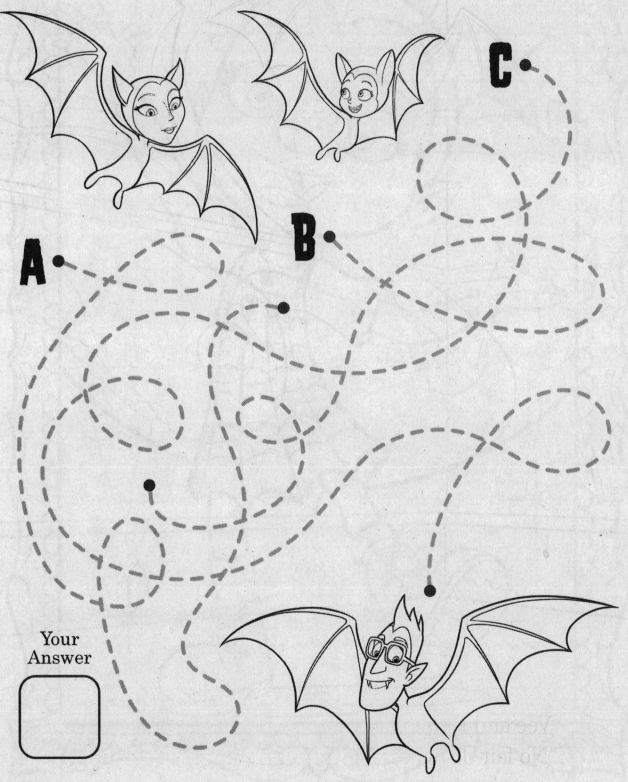

Your
Answer

TIC-TAC-TOE

SPOOKY SQUARES

Example

Taking turns, connect a line from one dot to another. Whoever make the line that completes a box puts their initial inside the box. The person with the most squares at the end of the game wins!

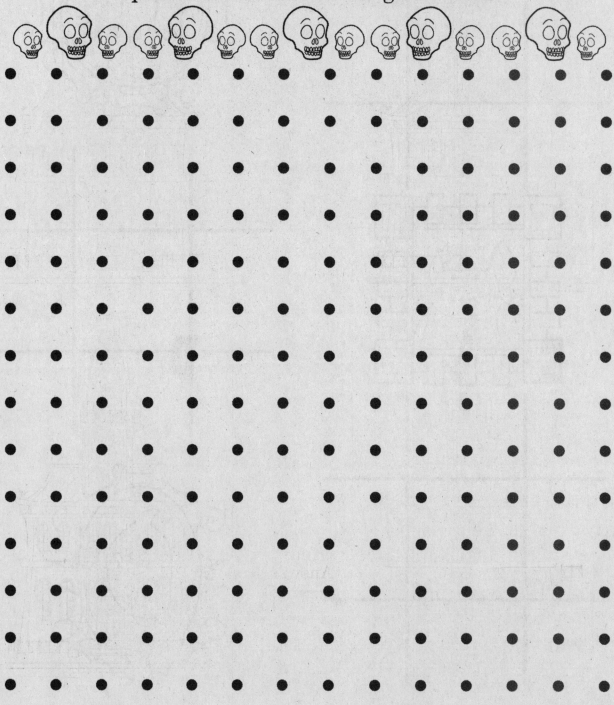

WHICH ARE THE SAME?

Which two images are the same?

A

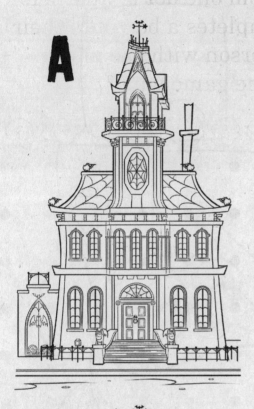

B

C

Your
Answer

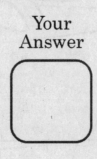

D

Vee meets Gregoria, the **GRUMPY** gargoyle.
She's lived in the house for hundreds of years!

FOLLOW THE PATH

Which path leads to Gregoria?

A.

B.

C.

Your
Answer

© Disney

PENELOPE

FOLLOW THE PATH

Which path leads to Vee?

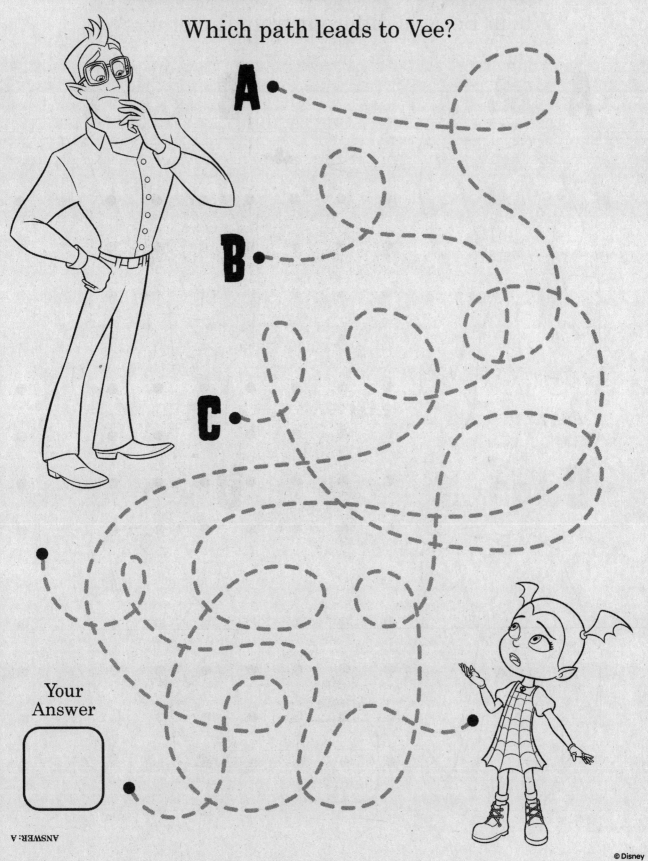

A

B

C

Your
Answer

© Disney

WHICH IS DIFFERENT?

Which Boris is different from the others?

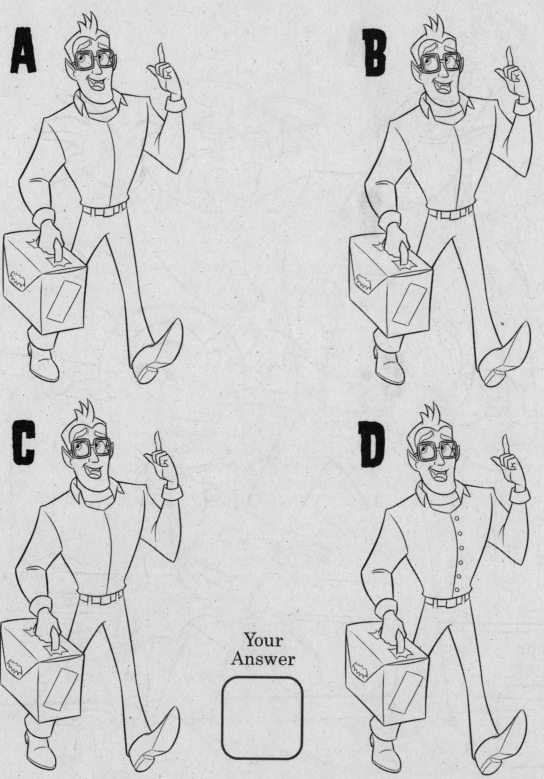

A

B

C

D

Your
Answer

"I can't wait to make more new friends," Vee cheers.
"Just remember love," Boris says. "Humans are a little jumpy."

BORIS

HOW MANY?

Count the vampires. How many do you see?

Your Answer

EEEKS! The doorbell starts to shriek.
The first visitor has arrived!

"WELCOME TO THE NEIGHBORHOOD!"
says Edna Peepleson.

She gives Oxana a bouquet of flowers.

Look down and across to find the flower names listed below.

```
X V P O P P Y U G Q
L I R N S E Z T M A
I O O B P T A H T W
L L S L A U G X J D
A E E U N N P C O A
C T X E S I J U C I
E Y Y B Y A N F I S
X Y W E A T Y M X Y
A L I L Y D A B X M
O T U L I P Z N W E
```

DAISY   **BLUEBELL**

ROSE   **LILY**

PETUNIA   **VIOLET**

TULIP   **POPPY**

PANSY   **LILAC**

Answer:

WHICH IS DIFFERENT?

Which Edna is different from the others?

A

B

C

D

Your Answer

Edna meets Penelope the man-eating plant.
"AAHHHHH!!!" she screams.

"You're right, Dad," Vee says. "Humans are jumpy."

FOLLOW THE PATH

Which path leads to the spider?

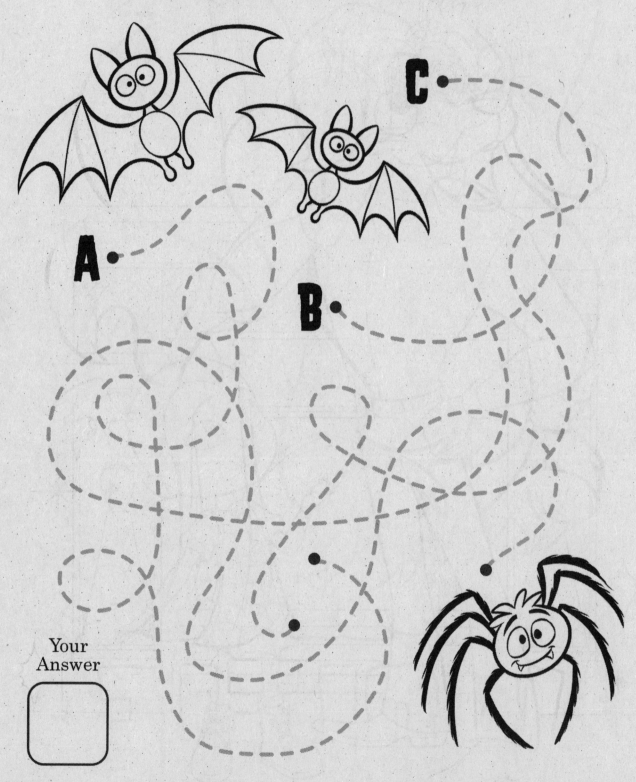

Your
Answer

WOLFIE

Draw a picture of your family.

SPOOKY SQUARES

Example

Taking turns, connect a line from one dot to another. Whoever make the line that completes a box puts their initial inside the box. The person with the most squares at the end of the game wins!

SHADOW MATCH

Which shadow matches Boris?

A

B

C

Your Answer

"What if I don't make any friends in Pennsylvania?" she worries.

"Let's show the whole human world how lovable you are!" Demi says.

Which picture of Vee and Demi is different?

A

B

C

D

EDNA

Using the grid as a guide, draw the character in the box below.

MISSING PIECE

Circle the missing piece of the puzzle.

1

2

3

"Hi! I'm Poppy," the girl next door says.
"This is my brother Edgar."

"And I'm Bridget!" another girls says.

"I'm Vampirina," says Vee. "I just moved in."

WHICH ARE THE SAME?

Which two images are the same?

A

B

C

Your
Answer
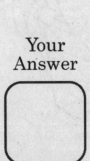

D

© Disney

SHADOW MATCH

Which shadow matches Penelope?

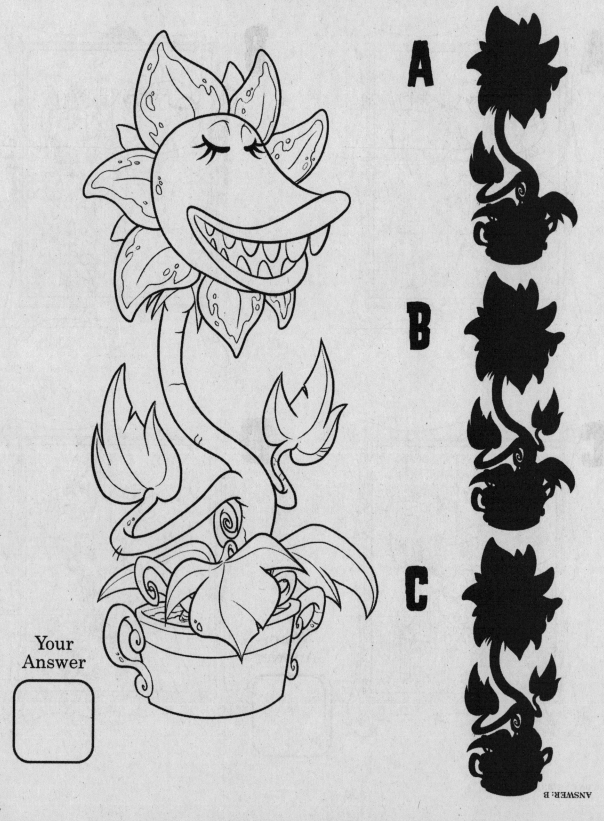

A

B

C

Your
Answer

ANSWER: B

WHICH ARE THE SAME?

Which two images are the same?

A

B

C

D

Your Answer

HOW MANY?

Count the pumpkins. How many do you see?

Your
Answer

"Edgar thinks your house is **HAUNTED**," Poppy admits.

SHADOW MATCH

Which shadow matches Edgar?

A

B

C

Your Answer

Help Vee lead Poppy and Edgar to her house.

Answer:

"Hello new friends!" Boris and Oxana cheer, surprising Poppy and Edgar.

"WELCOME!"

HOW MANY?

Count the spiders. How many do you see?

Your
Answer

Vee and Poppy race to Vee's room to play.

SHADOW MATCH

Which shadow matches Poppy?

A

B

C

Your
Answer

ANSWER: A

"MEET THE SCREAM GIRL DOLLS!"
Franken-Stacey, Ghastly Gayle and Creepy Caroline.

THE SCREAM GIRL DOLLS

How many words can you make
from the letters in The Scream Girl Dolls?

_____   _____

_____   _____

_____   _____

_____   _____

_____   _____

_____   _____

_____   _____

_____

_____

_____

Can you find 10 bats hidden in this picture?

Answer:

SPOOKY SQUARES

Example

Taking turns, connect a line from one dot to another. Whoever make the line that completes a box puts their initial inside the box. The person with the most squares at the end of the game wins!

EDGAR

Using the grid as a guide, draw the character in the box below.

WHICH ARE THE SAME?

Which two images are the same?

A

B

C

D

Your
Answer

GREGORIA

TIC-TAC-TOE

FOLLOW THE PATH

Which path leads to Bridget?

Your Answer

"HUMAN!"

Demi shouts when he sees Poppy.

"GHOST!"

Poppy shouts when she sees Demi.

MISSING PIECE

Circle the missing piece of the puzzle.

1

2

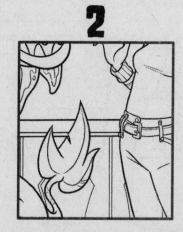

3

ANSWER: 2

MAN-EATING PLANT

How many words can you make
from the letters in Man-Eating Plant?

_____

_____

_____

_____

_____

_____

_____

_____

_____

_____

At the end of each row, circle the correct picture to finish the pattern.

Answer:

"It's just me, Vampirina," Vee says.

"AH HA!" Edgar says. "I knew something strange was going on in here!"

FOLLOW THE PATH

Which path leads to Edgar?

Your
Answer

© Disney

WORD SEARCH

Look up, down, and across for the words listed below.

V	F	L	S	P	I	D	E	R	S
A	A	S	T	R	A	N	G	E	P
M	O	M	F	I	E	I	N	G	O
P	B	O	P	D	S	G	U	H	O
I	A	A	R	I	J	H	L	O	K
R	T	E	D	E	R	T	D	S	Y
E	S	D	U	T	A	I	E	T	P
S	L	G	M	Z	H	F	N	R	E
Y	C	R	E	E	P	Y	R	A	S
H	A	U	N	T	E	D	N	A	M

BATS   **SPIDERS**

CREEPY   **SPOOKY**

GHOST   **STRANGE**

HAUNTED   **VAMPIRES**

NIGHT   **VAMPIRINA**

© Disney

"I screamed because we both
love Justin Teether!" Poppy says.

"I wanted to be your friend before you turned into a bat," Poppy tells Vee.

"Why wouldn't I want to be your friend afterwards, too?"

Draw a picture of your favorite toy.

JUSTIN TEETHER

How many words can you make
from the letters in Justin Teether?

_____   _____

_____   _____

_____   _____

_____   _____

_____   _____

_____

_____

_____

Vee has a new friend, and the Hauntleys are settled
in Philadelphia. Now Oxana can open the bed and
breakfast she's always dreamed about: the Scare B&B!

Help Vee match the right family portrait to each picture frame.

Answer:

"Mama, I'll post the Scare B&B online!" Vee says.

WHICH IS DIFFERENT?

Which Vee is different from the others?

A

B

C

D

Your Answer

© Disney

SPOOKY SQUARES

Example

Taking turns, connect a line from one dot to another. Whoever make the line that completes a box puts their initial inside the box. The person with the most squares at the end of the game wins!

MISSING PIECE

Circle the missing piece of the puzzle.

1

2

3

Boris has plans for the new house, too.
He invited the Peeplesons to stay for the night!

"What's the worst that could happen!" Oxana wonders.

© Disney

WHICH IS DIFFERENT?

Which Bridget is different from the others?

A

B

C

Your
Answer

D

TIC-TAC-TOE

Two more guests show up at the front door!
Cosmina and Narcisa are 900-year-old vampire sisters.

Draw a picture of the Hauntley house during the day in
the top box. Draw a picture of the Hauntley house at night
in the bottom box.

HOW MANY?

Count the cauldrons. How many do you see?

Your
Answer

SHADOW MATCH

Which shadow matches Gregoria?

Your
Answer

A B C

"Since vampires sleep during the day and humans sleep at night, they won't need the room at the same time!" Vee says.

VAMPIRINA

Using the grid as a guide, draw the character in the box below.

WHICH ARE THE SAME?

Which two images are the same?

A

B

C

D

Your
Answer

Narcisa and Cosmina use the guest room first.
They spread on green frog slime masks before they go to bed.

Oxana makes lunch for the Peeplesons.

Circle all the vegetables you see.

Answer:

© Disney

TIC-TAC-TOE

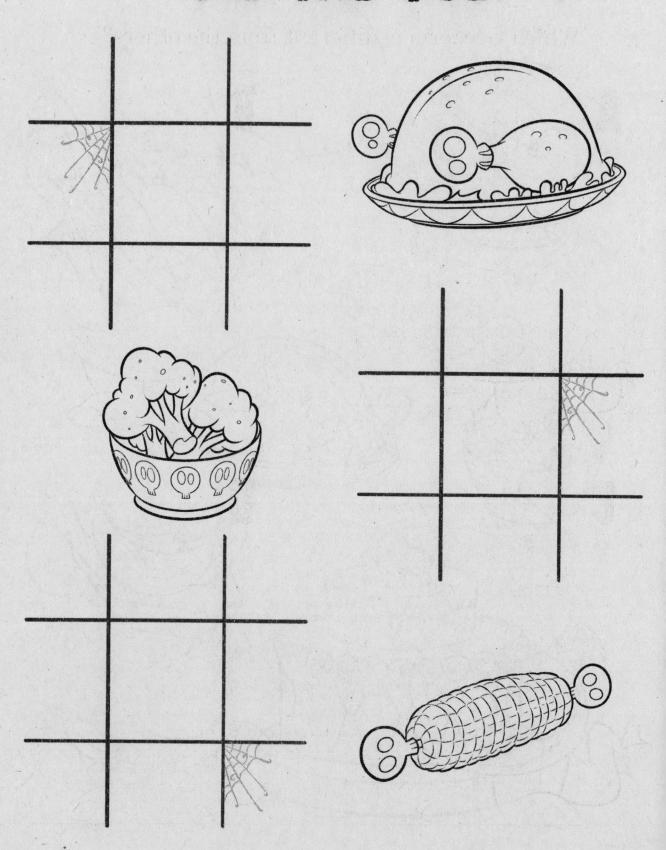

WHICH IS DIFFERENT?

Which Gregoria is different from the others?

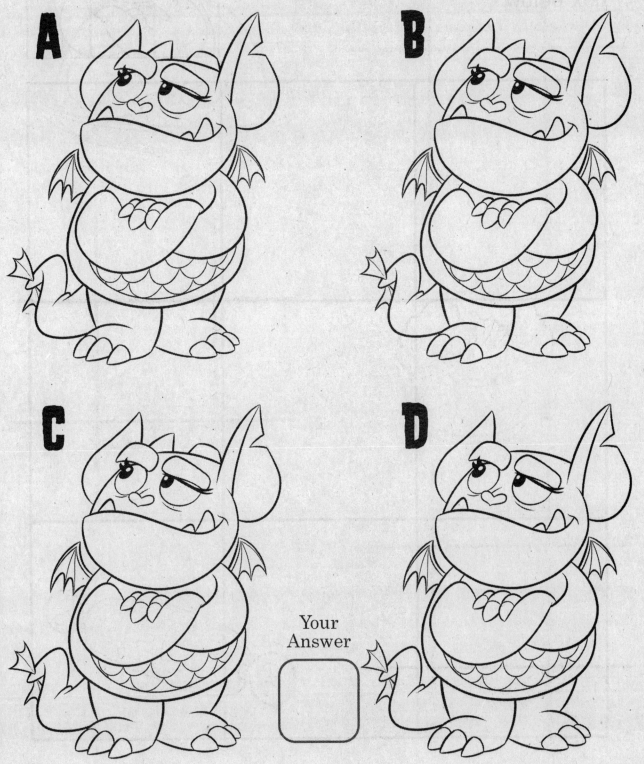

A

B

C

D

Your Answer

GREGORIA

Using the grid as a guide,
draw the character in the
box below.

VAMPIRE SISTERS

How many words can you make
from the letters in Vampire Sisters?

_____   _____

_____   _____

_____   _____

_____   _____

_____   _____

_____

_____

_____

_____

_____

MISSING PIECE

Circle the missing piece of the puzzle.

1

2

3

ANSWER: 1

TIC-TAC-TOE

SPOOKY SQUARES

Taking turns, connect a line from one dot to another. Whoever make the line that completes a box puts their initial inside the box. The person with the most squares at the end of the game wins!

© Disney

When the sun sets, it's time for the Peeplesons to get ready for bed.

That's when Vee wakes the vampire sisters up
and gives them a tour of the neighborhood.

HOW MANY?

Count the webs. How many do you see?

Your
Answer

"Did everything go okay?" Poppy asks when Vee gets back.
"Yep!" Vee replies. "But it's a good thing they're leaving
in the morning!"

Is that…

...Poppy's mom with Narcisa and Cosmina?
IT IS!

All that yoga has made the vampire sisters hungry.
Edna whips up some of her famous blood sausages for them.

FOLLOW THE PATH

Which path leads to Narcisa?

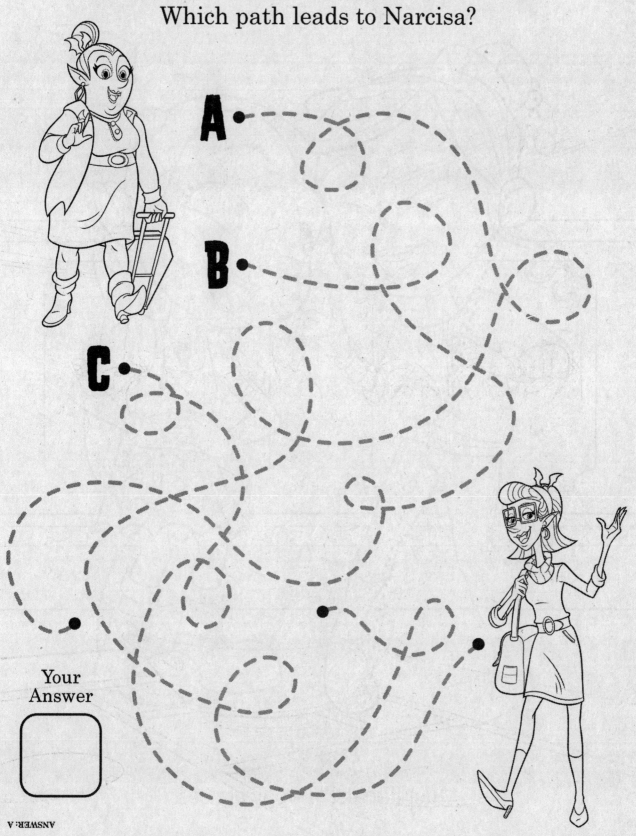

A.

B.

C.

Your Answer

© Disney

"Looks like your mom and our vampire guests
have a lot in common!" Vee says.

"Just like us!" Poppy agrees.

TIC-TAC-TOE

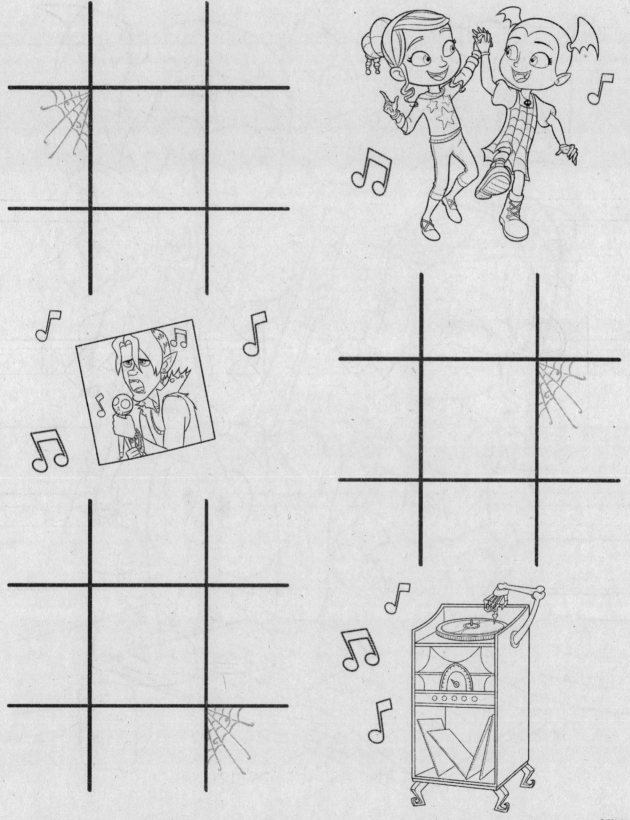

Poppy helps Vee get ready for her first day of school!

Vampirina's name starts with the letter V.
Circle four things in the picture that also begin with V.

Answer:

© Disney

Vee goes to school with a plant for her new teacher.

POPPY

Using the grid as a guide, draw the character in the box below.

"SMILE!" Mr. Gore says.

"I have an idea!" Poppy says.

Poppy painted a portrait of her best friend!

Vee puts the painting on the class tree. "I think school
in Pennsylvania is going to be just fine," she says.

© Disney

Poppy, Bridget, and Vee are best friends.

Happy Day!

"What shall I wear?"

Daisy is looking lovely.

BLING!

Look up, down, across, and diagonally
for these fun, sparkly blings.

BEADS **BRACELET** **NECKLACE**
BELT **GEM** **PURSE**
BOWS **JEWEL** **RING**

R	❋	B	O	W	S	B	N
I	T	O	J	E	W	E	L
N	⚬	N	A	S	C	A	B
G	E	M	❋	K	I	D	E
W	F	D	L	P	⚬	S	L
B	R	A	C	E	L	E	T
H	C	⚬	V	J	B	❋	A
E	R	B	P	U	R	S	E

Minnie loves a bit of bling.
Draw some of your favorite pieces of jewelry.

How sparkly!

"Look at my new ring!"

Minnie is ready to go shopping!.

Daisy

Super cute!

Be happy!

Can you think of five words that rhyme with **BLING?** Write (or have someone else write) the words.

POSSIBLE ANSWERS: bring, cling, ding, fling, ping, ring, sing, sting, string, thing, wing

Donald

© Disney

Butterflies look like bows.

Happy Day!

Scooter Girl

Garden Gala

Splish, splash!

Daisy is growing daisies!

More to share!

Help Mickey find Minnie.

Summer blooms!

Draw what Goofy is thinking about.

© Disney

Minnie

funny bunny

Draw what Daisy is thinking about.

© Disney

What a cutie!

Let's have a
tea party

A purse adds a pop of color.

Minnie and Daisy love to shop!
Draw your favorite dress or outfit.

Help Minnie design the perfect outfit.

Color the dress, purse, and shoes.

Minnie loves her pets!
Draw a picture of your favorite animal.

Figaro

Nose to nose.

Rocker Chick!

Cuckoo-Loca plays for Figaro.

Who Am I?

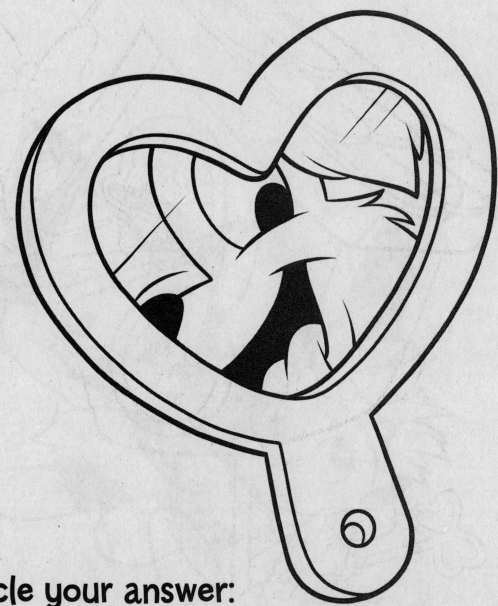

Circle your answer:

Figaro

Clarabelle

Shelby

Cuckoo-Loca

Home Sweet Home

Bath Time

The bubbles are everywhere!

Which one is different?

Shelby

Pluto's Bow

Find and circle 4 differences in the two pictures.

Answers: Minnie's tail is missing, the leash is missing, spots on the dog are missing, Minnie's button is missing.

Lollipop

"A pretty bow for you!"

How sweet!

Looking good!

Animal Friends

How lovely!

A pretty little pet!

Rainy Day

Rainbow!

It's playtime!

Let's take a road trip!

Better Together

Connet the dots
to see what Minnie is growing.

Twirly Girl

Tweet-tweet-tweet!

So Cute!

Spring Flowers

Find and circle the springtime words.

FLOWER   **SPRING**
KITE   **RAIN**
RIBBON   **RAINBOW**

```
K L R I B B O N I
I E O E G R P S
T Y H Z Q A H F
E S P R I N G L
T S T A C I G O
S R A I N B O W
B J E N K T A E
A G T N O W B R
```

Goofy

Which piece completes the picture?

A

B

C

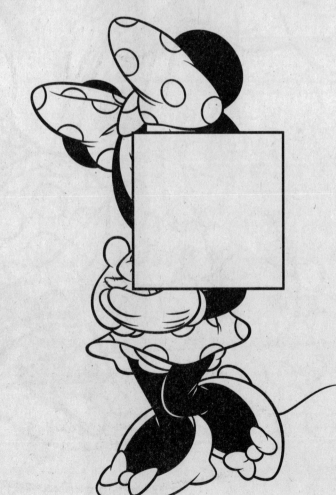

Your Answer:

Sweet as Springtime!

Picture Perfect

© Disney

Better Together

Make a list of things you love.

I Love . . .

_____

_____

_____

_____

_____

_____

_____

_____

A bicycle built for two!

© Disney

Happy Day!

Hello, little butterfly.

Count each object.
How many are in each group?
Match the number to the
correct number of objects.

1

2

3

4

5

Draw some yummy picnic foods!

Fresh fruit from the garden!

Daisy likes cupcakes.

Decorate the cupcake!

What a surprise!

Help Minnie, Melody, and Millie get to the picnic table.

Start

Finish

Summer Picnic

Sweet Treat!

A wonderful day for friends to play.

Ready to soar!

Such pretty kites!

Draw a new kite for Minnie.

"What a beautiful day!"

kites
are flowers in the
sky

© Disney

KITE DANCERS

Breezy Day

"A pretty bow for me!"

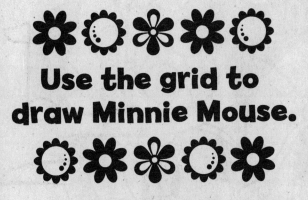

Use the grid to draw Minnie Mouse.

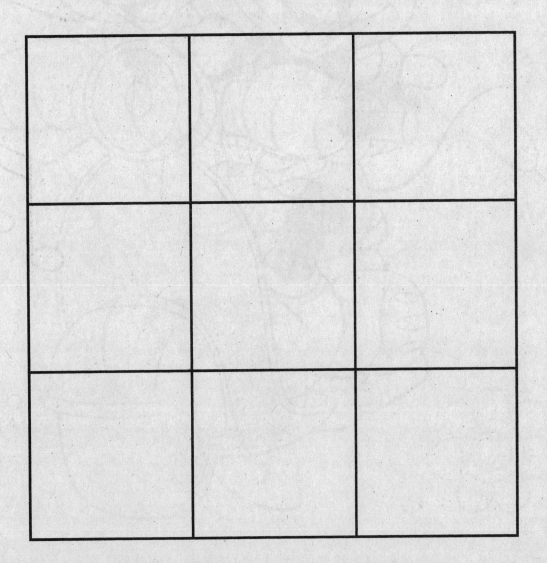

Time for an adventure!

Mickey and Minnie pal around all day. Draw pictures of their silly afternoon.

at the park . . .

eating a snack . . .

© Disney

I'm ready to roll!

Where shall we go?

What is Minnie
thinking of?

SHOPPING SPREE!

You've won a shopping spree at your favorite store. Draw some cool things you would buy.

Minnie writes and draws
in her diary every day.
What would you draw
in your diary?

Dear Diary,
This is what I did today.

Minnie likes cheering for her friends.
Create a cheer for Minnie, and have
someone write it here.

_____

_____

_____

_____

_____

_____

_____

"Butterflies look like bows!"

Minnie loves butterflies.
Draw and color a beautiful butterfly!

Friendship warms the heart.

Say, cheese.

Circle 3 pictures of
flowers and 4 suns.

Fun in the sun!

Puppy Love

Sweetheart Minnie

Decode the sign by matching letters to the shapes.

A B _ W   F _ R
♡   ♡

_ V _ RY
⋈ ⋈

_ _ A _ _ N!
⬡ ⋈ ⬡ ♡

Use this key to decode the sign.

 =E   =S   ♡ =O

So many to pick from!

It's bow-making time

Cuckoo-Loca

Let's make some bows!

Little Helpers

Helping Hands

What fun!

Making mischief!

Oops!

Minnie's newest bows!

How many bow ties do you count?

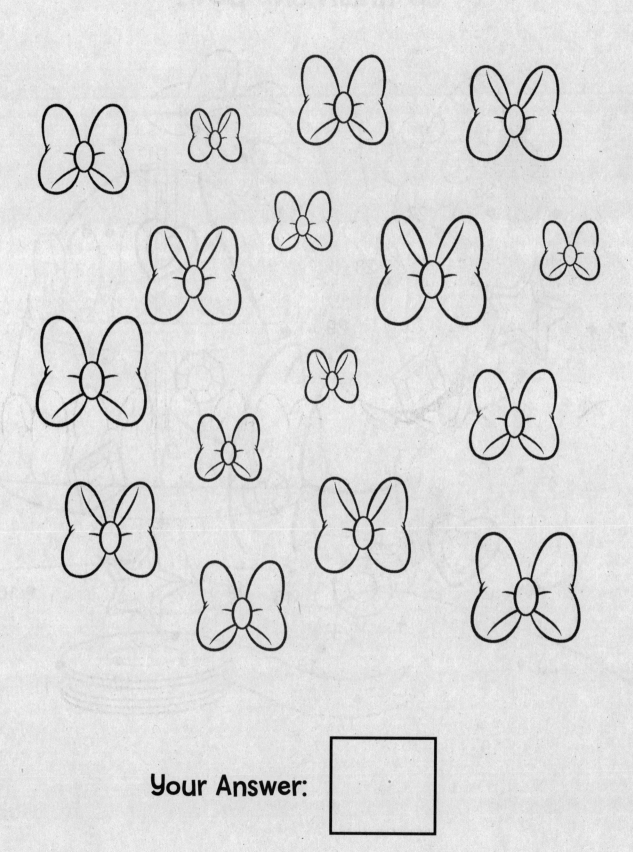

Your Answer:

Connect the dots
to finish the bow.

Superstar Penelope Poodle!

Going to the Dance!

Unscramble
the words.

SOWB ___ ___ ___ ___

NEINMI ___ ___ ___ ___ ___ ___

RNOBIB ___ ___ ___ ___ ___ ___

SAYID ___ ___ ___ ___ ___

EDASB ___ ___ ___ ___ ___

Looking good!

Busy Day

There's no business like bow business!

Bows are Minnie's favorite accessory!
Color the bows.

Follow the leaky pipes to Clarabelle.

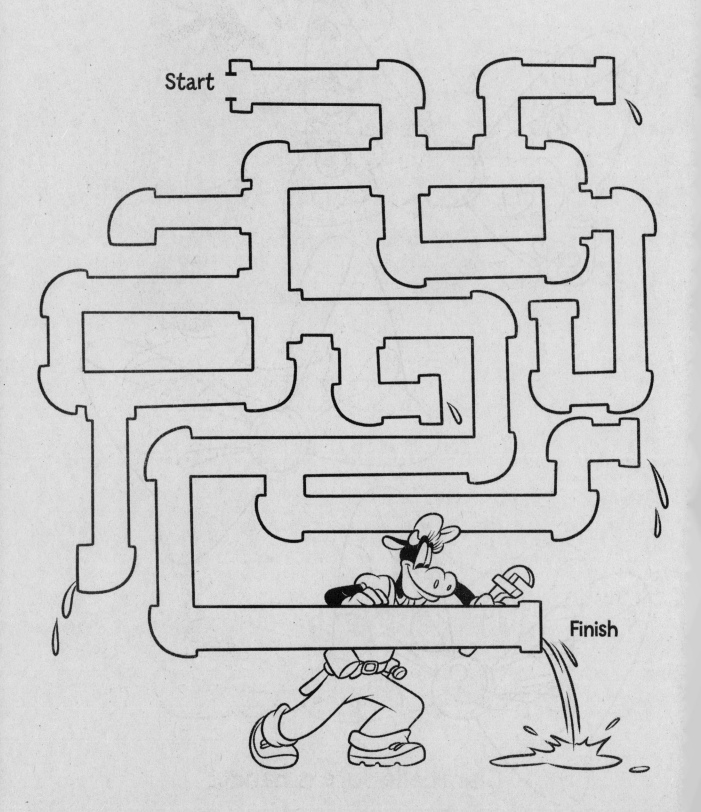

Clarabelle sure is handy!

Help Daisy
with her drawing.

Oops! It's bathtime!

What numbers come next in the patterns?

A 3 2 1   3 2 1   3 _ _

B 7 0 7   0 7 0   7 _ _

C 4 4 4   2 2 2   4 _ _

Figaro

Suppertime!

Which Minnie is different?

Answer: C

What does Figaro see?
Connect the dots to find out!

Wake up, Donald...

... It's time for breakfast!

Better Together

Find and circle the words listed below.

FALL **LEAF**
FIGARO **HEARTS**
BOW

F I G A R O O
A G B A C B
L B R B O W
L E A F A E
L S P D Q K
H E A R T S

Friends and fun forever!

JUMBO
Coloring & Activity Book

By Steve Behling

bendon®

The BENDON name, logo and
Tear and Share are trademarks of
Bendon, Ashland, OH 44805.

Here's Mickey in his Daily Driver.

But it can transform into a supercool roadster!

His pals have roadsters, too!

© Disney

Draw a line from each racer to the matching roadster!

Answer:

Mickey burns up the road in his roadster!

Mickey and Donald like to race.

They help each other get ready.

Can you find and circle the only tire that will fit Donald's roadster?

Answer:

Look at Donald go!

Connect the dots to see what Donald's driving now.

© Disney

"Welcome to the Race for the Rigatoni Ribbon!"

"Rigatoni Racers . . . rev up! Get set! Go!"

Piston Pietro thinks he can beat
Donald and the roadster racers.

It's the old "Pizza Pie Flip-and-Fly."
Piston Pietro is cheating!

"I've got your back, Minnie!"

© Disney

Find and cross out all the pizzas.

Answer:

Goofy loves pizza!

Help Goofy and Piston Pietro find their way to the finish line.

Start

Finish

"ROCKIN' AND RACIN'!"

"WINNING IN STYLE!"

"CRUISIN' THROUGH!"

"LIFE IN THE FASHION LANE!"

Pete is pals with Mickey.

But he has a lot to learn about being a good sport!

Can you match Pete to the right shadow?

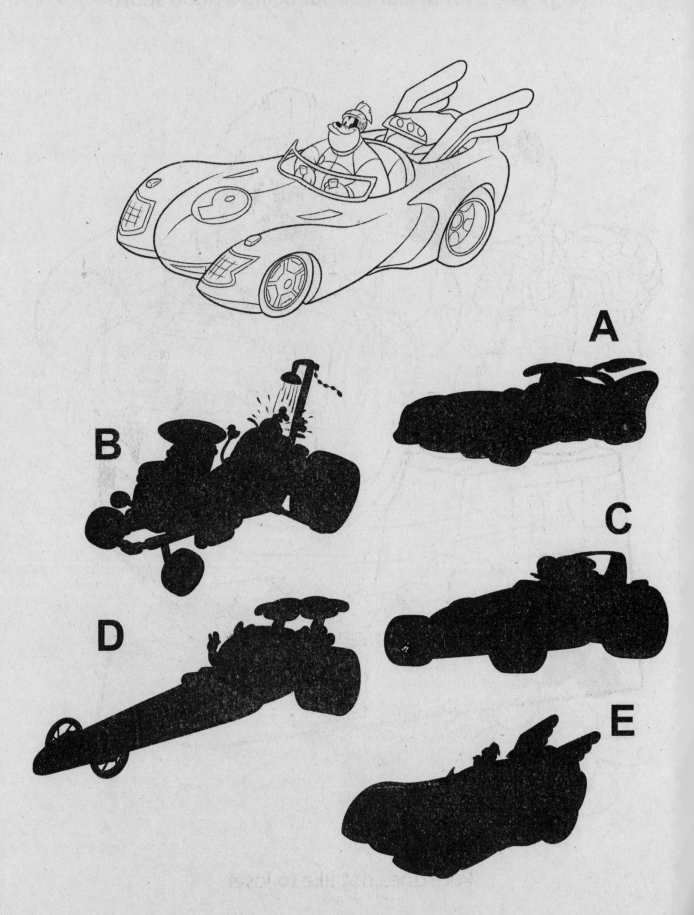

A

B

C

D

E

Pete does not like to lose!

Sometimes Pete breaks the rules
because he wants so badly to win.

Help Pete follow the trail of hot dogs up, down, left, and right to find Goofy. Don't step on any oil slicks!

Start

Finish

Answer:

Pete is not always nice, but sometimes
he does the right thing!

Pete learns to race for fun, not just to win.

Which piece completes this Pete puzzle?

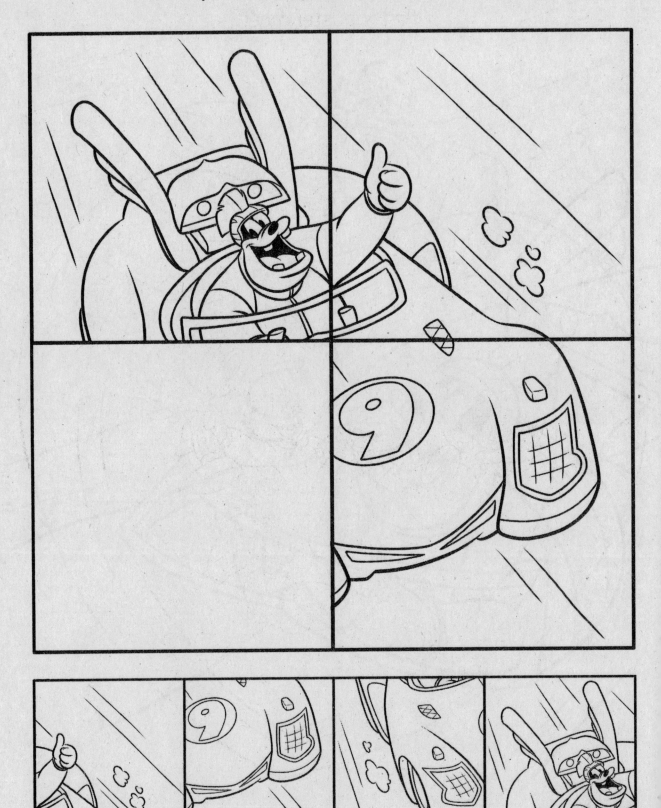

A. B. C. D.

Answer: C

It's the anniversary of Mickey and Minnie's first roadster race!

Meanwhile, sneaky Sir Lord Pete
takes the Queen's Royal Ruby.

Circle the missing Royal Ruby to help the police officer!

Answer:

© Disney

Sir Lord Pete tosses the Royal Ruby
before he can be caught!

"A raceversary gift? For me?"

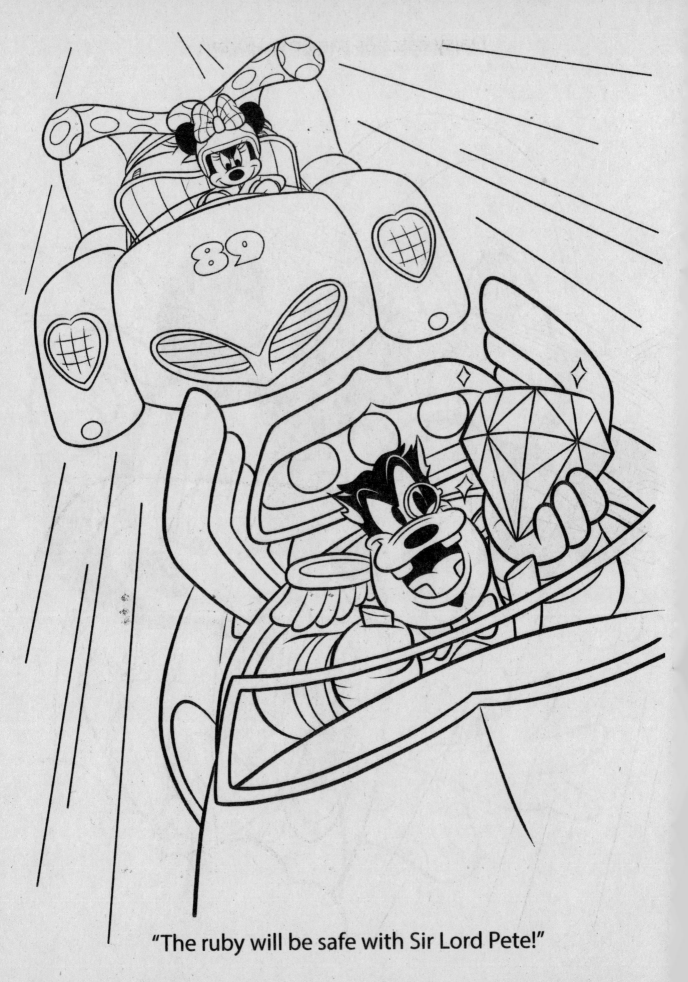

"The ruby will be safe with Sir Lord Pete!"

Daisy catches the Royal Ruby!

Find the path that leads to Goofy and keeps the Royal Ruby away from Sir Lord Pete!

Answer: D

"ROADSTER READY"

"You're all washed up, Sir Lord Pete!"

Put the picture in order to tell the story!

A

B

C

D

Draw a line to match each Daily Driver with its Roadster Racer mode.
Don't forget to pick up the driver along the way!

Answers:

The Roadster Racers drive all around the world.

They love to race!

Think Donald is driving an ordinary car?
Donald's Daily Driver can become...

...his Cabin Cruiser. **Splash!**

Pick a roadster, and find your way to the trophy!

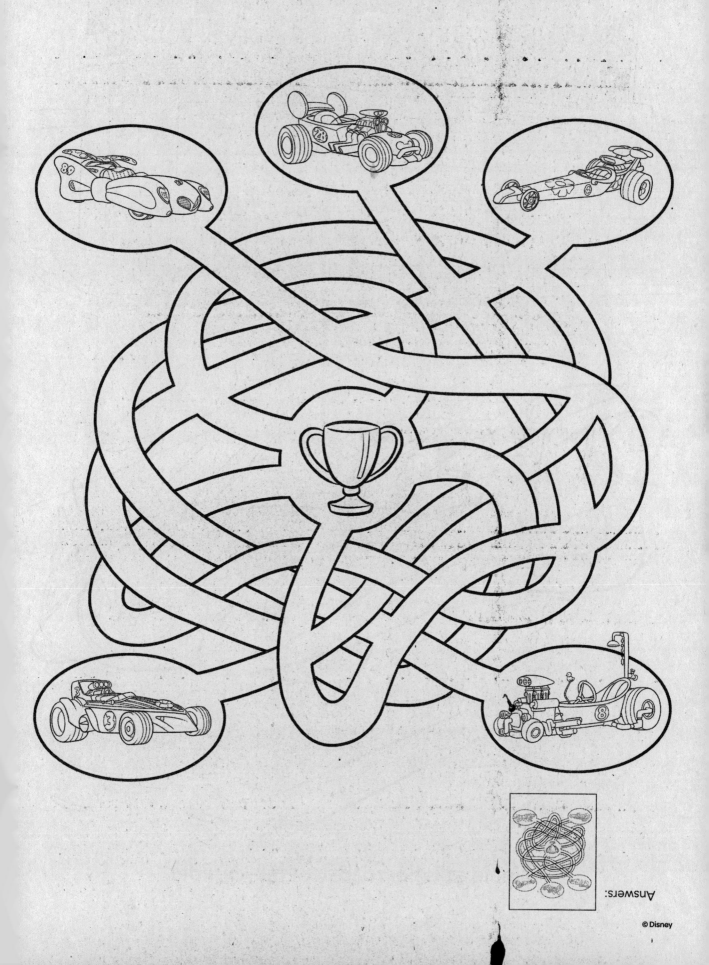

Minnie calls her roadster Pink Thunder.

Daisy drives the stylish Snapdragon.

Goofy can drive **and** shower in the Turbo Tubster!

"I've heard there's so much to do in Madrid!"

"Team Mickey on the go!"

Disney PUPPY DOG PALS

Written by Steve Behling

Meet Bingo . . .

. . . and Rolly!

Which shadow matches Bingo?

A

B

C

Use the grid to draw Rolly.

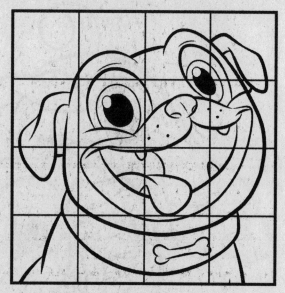

© Disney

They do all the usual dog things . . .

. . . and some not-so-usual dog things, too!

How many balls do you count?

How many words can you rhyme with
BALL

A.R.F. is a robot dog Bob created to help the pups.
He can do almost anything!

Connect the dots to see who will clean up the pups mess

Who is who?

Match each character to their name.

1

CUPCAKE

2

A.R.F.

3

BULWORTH

4

RUFUS

Answer: 1-Bulworth, 2-Cupcake, 3-Rufus, 4-A.R.F.

Create Your Own A.R.F

A.R.F. is an Auto-Doggie Robotic Friend.
If you had a robotic dog friend what would they look like?
Draw your friend below.

What are Bingo and Rolly zipping over?
Connect the dots to find out!

Bingo and Rolly live with their owner, Bob.

© Disney

Find the picture that is different.

A

B

C

D

Which line leads Bingo to Rolly?

Meet Bulworth. He teaches Bingo and Rolly
things that help with their missions.

"Junkyard dogs know everything!"

This is the pups' kitty sister, Hissy.

Help Bingo and Rolly unscramble the words below!

G O N I B

_ _ _ _ _

L O L Y R

_ _ _ _ _

O B B

_ _ _

S H Y S I

_ _ _ _ _

© Disney

The pups carry cool gadgets inside their collars.

Circle the gadgets Bingo and Rolly can use to cross the river.

© Disney

How many cars do you count?

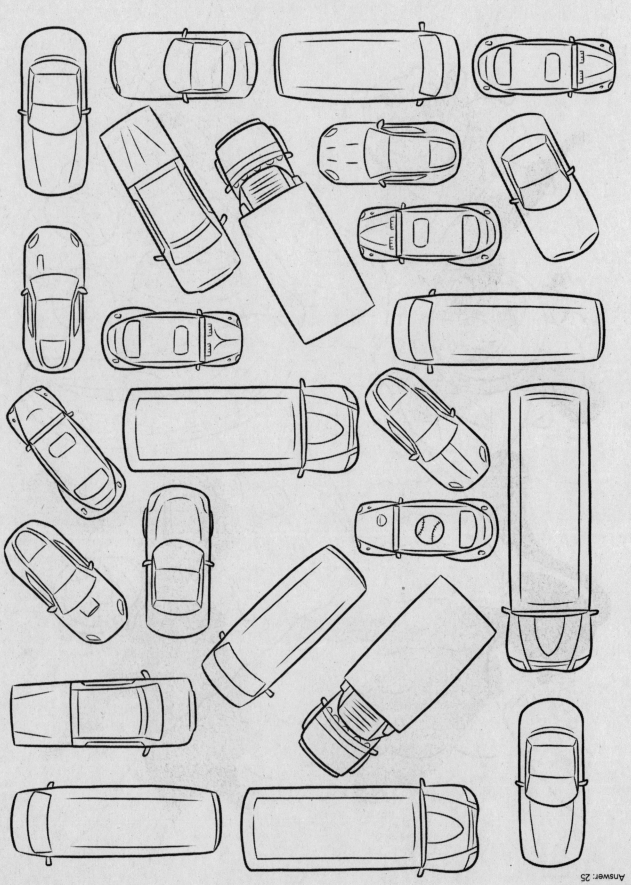

Answer: 25

Which shadow matches Hissy?

A

B

C

"Do you have to make such a mess, Bingo?"

"I can't make French toast without bread!"

"If I can't have French toast,
I get as grumpy as a bear!"

Going on a mission!

Crack the Code

Using the secret code below, fill in
the blanks and reveal the hidden words.

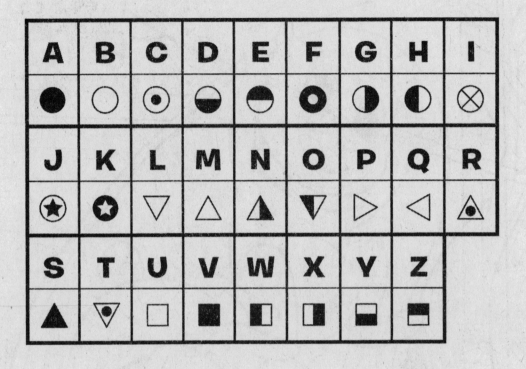

Have an adult cut out the puzzle pieces on the dotted lines.
Mix up the pieces, and put the picture back together!

LARGE And small
Color all of the SMALL pictures of Bob.

Word Scramble

Unscramble the letters to correctly
spell the names and words.

HOGDOSUE

BLOLVAE

EUCESR

AHGN UPP

Answer: doghouse, lovable, rescue, hang pup

© Disney

Help Bingo and Rolly find the path that leads to the slide!

The pups look for bread to make
French toast—in France!

Sector Grid

Use the small grid to help complete the picture.

Crack the Code

Using the secret code below, fill in
the blanks and reveal the hidden words.

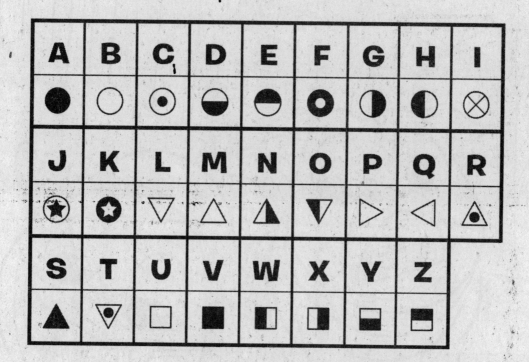

___ ___ ___

___ ___ ___ ___ ___ ___ ___

"Stop, in the name of the paws!"

Which line should Bingo follow to stop the mice from getting away?

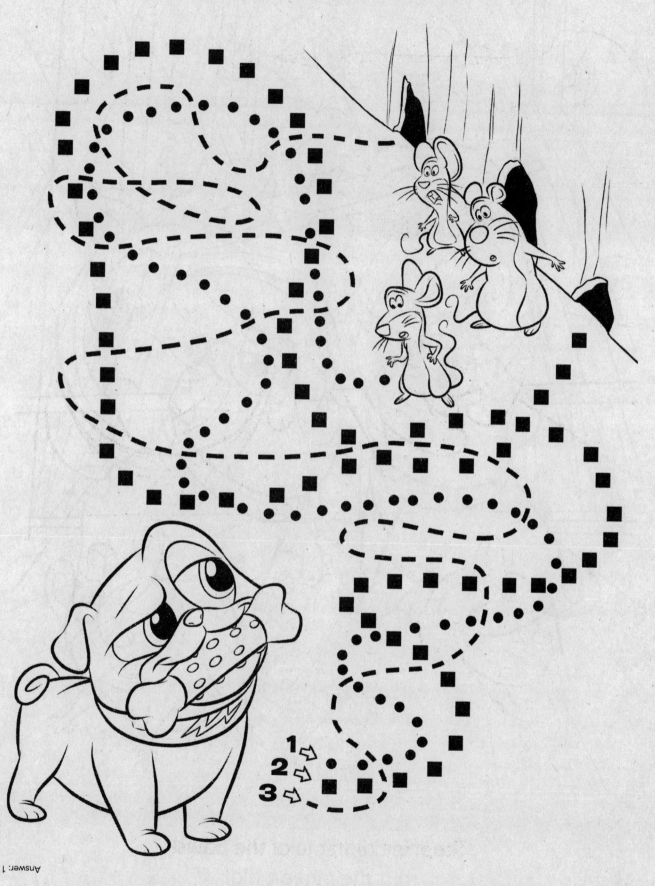

1
2
3

The mice didn't take the bread,
but the pigeon did!

Circle what's wrong with this picture?

© Disney

Finish the picture of Frank.

Secret Message

Cross out the words RUFUS every time you see it in the box.
When you reach a letter that does not belong, write it
in the spaces below to reveal the secret message.

RUFUSHRUFUSRUF
USRUFUSIRUFUSR
UFUSGRUFUSRUFU
SRUFUSRUFUSHRU
FUSRUFUSRUFUSR
UFUSPRUFUSRUFU
SRUFUSRUFUSARU
FUSRUFUSRUFUSW
RUFUSRUFUSRUFUS

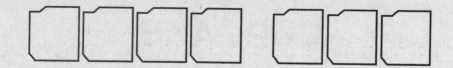

Extreme Close-up
Can you guess who this is?

ESTHER
CUPCAKE
HISSY

Follow The Path

Using the letters, in order, from the name HISSY,
follow the correct path to find your way through the maze.

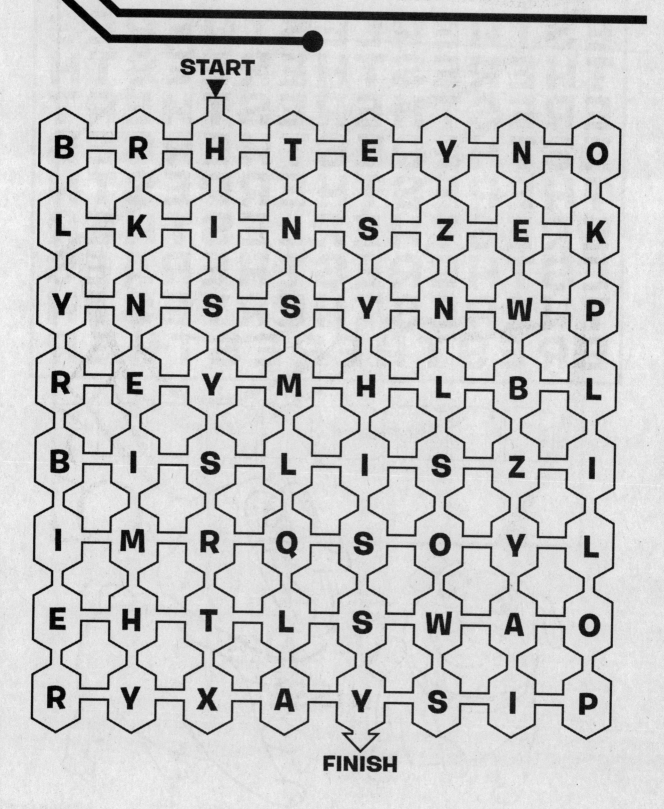

START

FINISH

© Disney

Secret Message

Cross out the words ESTHER every time you see it in the box.
When you reach a letter that does not belong, write it
in the spaces below to reveal the secret message.

```
ESTHERLESTHERES
THERESTHEREESTH
ERESTHERESTHERT
ESTHERESTHERSES
THERESTHERPESTH
ERESTHERLESTHER
ESTHERESTHERAES
THERESTHERYESTH
ERESTHERESTHER
```

☐ ☐ ☐ ' ☐   ☐ ☐ ☐ ☐

Sector Grid

Use the small grid to help complete the picture.

Cupcake thinks she's the boss
of everyone. Especially Rufus!

"Isn't Rufus a big ol' meanie, Bingo?"

Finish the picture of Rufus.

Sector Grid

Use the small grid to help complete the picture.

LARGE And small
Color all of the LARGE pictures of Cupcake.

Crack the Code

Using the secret code below, fill in
the blanks and reveal the hidden words.

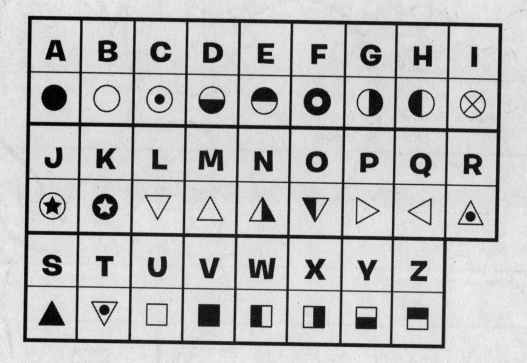

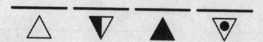

DISNEY PUPPY DOG PALS

The puppy dog pals love going on missions. Describe what your fun mission would be like below.

_____

_____

_____

_____

_____

_____

_____

_____

_____